DEDICATION:

To Noelle who urged me to write a story just for the joy of it.
And to all the too tall, too small, too skinny, too fat, too smart,
too silly girls who deserve to see, really see, and love themselves.

Text Copyright © 2009 by Barbara Worton
Illustrations Copyright © by Dom Rodi

Published in the United States by
Great Little Books, LLC

Great Little Books, LLC books are distributed by
Midpoint Trade Books, Inc.

Publisher's Cataloging-In-Publication Data

Worton, Barbara.
Too tall Alice / by Barbara Worton ; illustrations by Dom Rodi.

p. : ill. ; cm.

Summary : A story about all too tall, too small, too skinny, too fat, too
smart and too silly girls who deserve to see, really see, and love themselves.
ISBN: 978-0-9790661-1-5

1. Girls--Juvenile fiction. 2. Self-perception--Juvenile fiction. 3. Self-esteem--Juvenile
fiction. 4. Girls--Fiction. I. Rodi, Dom. II. Title.

PZ7.W6786 Too 2009
[Fic]

Printed in China

www.greatlittlebooksllc.com

TOO TALL ALICE

By Barbara Worton

Illustrations by Dom Rodi

Great Little Books, LLC

ALICE IS TALL. NOT T-REX, EMPIRE STATE BUILDING TALL.
NOT EVEN AS TALL AS HER DAD.
JUST MAYBE FOUR INCHES TALLER
THAN THE OTHER EIGHT-YEAR-OLD
GIRLS AT THE
CHERRY TREE SCHOOL TALL.

ME!

MOM

DOC!

"FOUR EXTRA INCHES TO LOVE," HER MOTHER
WOULD SAY AND KISS ALICE ON THE CHEEK.
"GOOD AND HEALTHY TALL. PERFECTLY
NORMAL," HER DOCTOR WOULD SAY.

"JUST TALL ENOUGH TO BE THE ONLY GIRL STANDING IN THE BACK ROW WITH THE BOYS FOR THE SCHOOL PHOTO," HER LITTLE ON THE SHORT AND FAT SIDE TEACHER WOULD SAY.

AND JUST TALL ENOUGH THAT ALL ALONE IN HER ROOM, ALICE WISHED SHE WAS FOUR INCHES SHORTER.

One night, Mom and Dad and their neighbors on the left and the right, on this and the other side of the street, were at Alice's house. It was card-party Friday!

Yippee!

It was the one night when the parents played their card games and the kids played their kid games.

It was the one night the kids ate tons of pizza, chocolates, chips and ran around until they were over-tired and over-fed –

grumpy kids

"slightly grumpy!"

scuff!

scrape!

and then the neighbors' kids marched grumpily home with their parents and into their beds, and Alice marched up to her room and into her super-fluffy Ariel the mermaid bed.

It was the one night when as soon as the parents were sure their kids were safe asleep in their beds, they came back to Alice's house and played cards until late, late, late at night.

Upstairs in her room, in her super-fluffy bed, Alice tried to lay down on the pillow and arrange her arms like a princess, sure that Prince Charming would come and find her and give her a kiss. Instead, Alice tossed and turned.

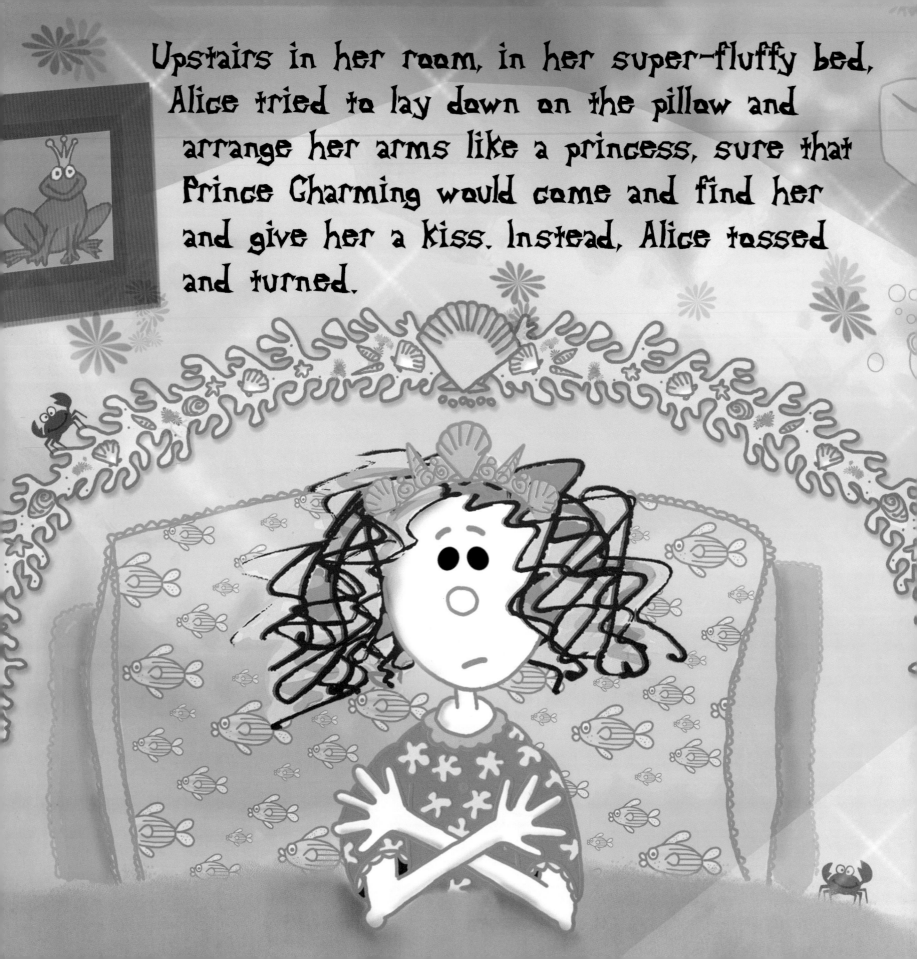

She could hear the s h u f f l i n g
of cards and the clinking of ice cubes.
She could hear the talk about
aching backs and lemon cars and
bosses that stink and kids that
don't do their homework and
repair projects that would happen
when some extra money came in.

Upstairs in her
super-fluffy bed,
trying so hard
to be a princess,
Alice sat up very
STRAIGHT.

Suddenly the card party voices dropped low - really low. She cupped her ears. She leaned toward the door. She strained to listen. But... She just heard, buzz, hum, buzz, hum, whisper, whisper, no,no,no,no,no,no, don't worry, don't worry, don't worry. Really.

Then BOOM-LOUD! She heard her father say, "She's going to be tall and thin, a string bean, a bean pole, a twig, a long drink of water, a toothpick."

"There's nothing wrong with being tall and THIN," she heard her neighbors say. "Look at those supermodels."

Everybody laughed. "Yeah, they're tall and stick thin, and making a bundle of money - more money than anybody in this room," she heard her neighbor's husband say.

"Yeah, maybe she'll be a supermodel," her other neighbor said. "God knows, we could use a bundle of money," she heard her mother say.

Alice cried. She didn't want to be a string bean. People ate string beans. She just wanted to be the same height as all the other eight-year-old girls in her class.

And Alice cried, and she cried, and she worried that
if she wasn't a bean pole that her parent's wouldn't
have enough money to keep a roof over her head,
and the rain would come in, and she would be
flooded in her super-fluffy bed and unable to
swim because she wasn't
Ariel the mermaid.

And Alice sniffed and she sniffled,

sniffle

sticky

and she wiped her sticky nose on the back of her hand.

YUK!

And her lip quivered and her eyes watered until she fell asleep –

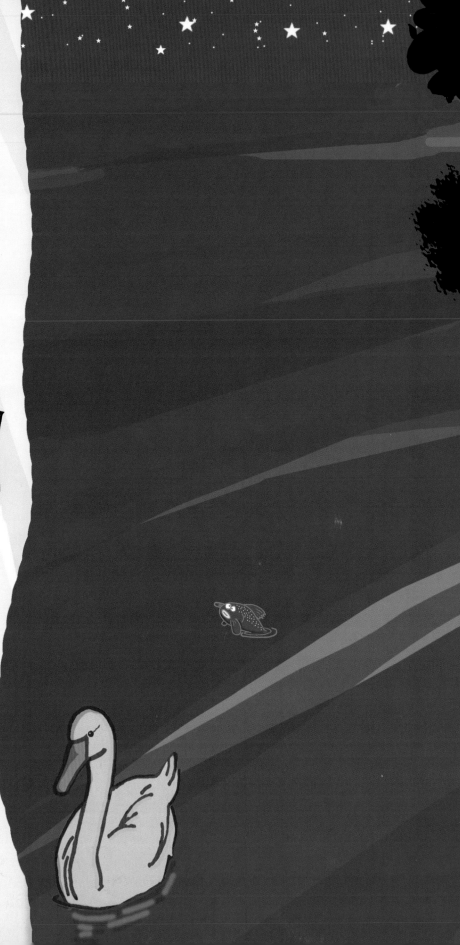

A breathless, **bumpy** sleep, dreaming that she was floating   on her super-fluffy bed, **drifting** down the street to the place where the **tall** girls lived.

Knock, Knock.

Alice tapped on an exceptionally tall wooden door.

"Who's there?" a very tall voice answered.

"Alice who's four inches taller than all the other eight-year-old girls at Cherry Tree School."

Clunk. Click. Rattle. Thump.

The security chain came off.
Alice walked in.
The room was huge -
three or four football fields huge.

The ceilings were high -
three or four basketball courts high.
And the room was filled with girls, all of them tall.

Basketball superstars

super models

circus show girl

There were tall enough to be basketball superstar girls.

There were tall enough to be supermodel girls.

There were tall enough to be circus sideshow girls.

There were girls who were tall enough to make Alice very nervous that she was already four inches taller than all the other eight-year-old girls at Cherry Tree School. Was she going to grow this tall?

So Alice cried, big, wet, sloppy, scared, miserable tears.

boo hoo!

"Hey, short-stuff," said two seven-foot-tall girls with a basketball, and they bent in half and gave Alice giant high-fives.

"Who are you calling short?" snapped Alice. "I'm four-inches taller than all the other eight-year-old girls at Cherry Tree School."

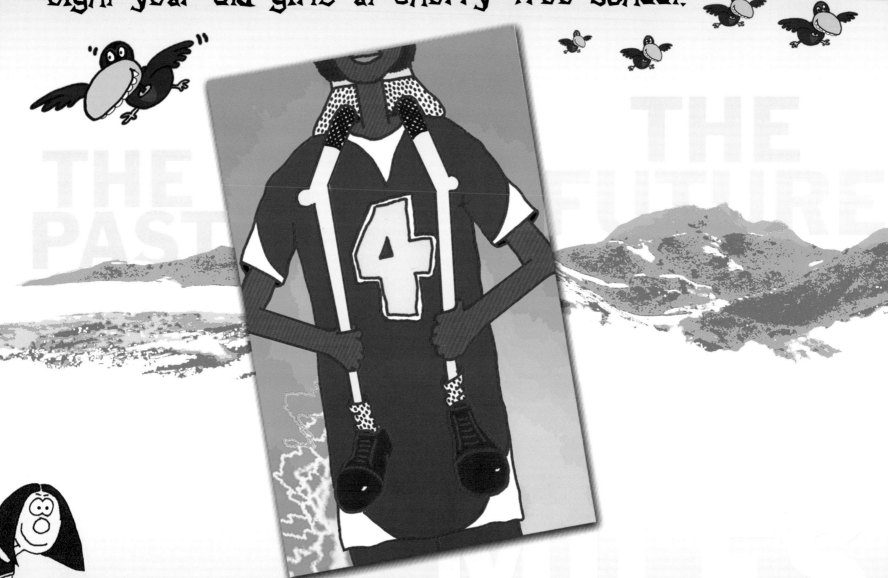

"But you're still at least three feet shorter than me," the girl with the basketball said and picked Alice up and put her on her shoulders.

Alice took a deep breath. The air was so clear way up – about 10-feet high. And she could see for miles and miles and miles. She could see way, way back, as far back as the past

and way, way ahead – as far ahead as the future. And she squinted and squinted, screwed up her eyes, her nose, made finger binoculars and looked ahead ten years into the future.

CHERRY TREE

Alice looked to the left and the right. She looked up and down. She saw her mother, her father, the boys in the back row and the girls in the front at her school. She saw her teacher, her doctor, her neighbors. But. But. But. Alice cried, "I don't see me."

UP

LEFT

"That's because you don't know who you're looking for," said the girl with the basketball. "You're not looking for you. Close your eyes. Open your heart, and you'll see yourself as clearly as I can see you."

"Help me," Alice said. "No," said the girl with the basketball. "You have to find yourself."

So, Alice closed her eyes.
Thump, thump, thump went
her eight-year-old, just the
right size heart. Swoosh
went the air around her
head up ten-feet high.
Then, Alice cheered, "I see
me! I see my blonde hair,
brown eyes and my extra
four-inches between my
head and my toes.
And I can feel my heart
thump, thump, thumping with
dreams."

Alice watched and listened
and like a movie on a giant
screen her heart told her
the story of all the
wonderful things she was
and all the wonderful
things she could be.

"This is a great story, and it's all about me," Alice said. "It's not about a string bean, a bean pole, a twig, a long drink of water or a toothpick. It's about me, the me only I can see."

"Are you too tall?" a voice asked.
"No," Alice said. "I'm just the right height for me."
And with a thump, thump, thump, Alice's heart let the credits roll:

And Alice heard the audience burst
into a **roar** of applause.

So, she turned around to take a bow,
And when she opened her eyes,
there she was, sitting up with her arms
stretched **wide,**

in her super-fluffy,
Ariel the mermaid bed,
and the sun was
shining in, a **big** smiling
sun with lots of teeth.
So, she gave a loud **yawn,**
stretched a huge **stretch**
and smiled from cheek to cheek.

Alice could see herself,
really see herself,
having a very beautiful day.